BELLE
the Last Mule at Gee's Bend

A CIVIL RIGHTS STORY

Calvin Alexander Ramsey & Bettye Stroud

illustrated by John Holyfield

CANDLEWICK PRESS

ALEX SAT ON A BENCH outside the store. He wanted to go and play, but his mother had told him to wait for her. There was nothing to do on the porch but watch an old mule eating in the garden across the street. There was no breeze. Not a leaf moved in the chinaberry trees. It was so still that Alex could hear the mule munching on a row of bright collard greens. He watched as the mule's big fuzzy ears twitched away a pesky fly.

An old woman walked slowly up the wooden steps to the store and sat down on the bench next to Alex. She fanned herself with a folded newspaper. He looked at her out of the corner of his eye. She was watching the mule, too.

The old woman chuckled and then said in a soft voice, "Myself, I like my collards cooked with some ham and spiced with vinegar."

Alex smiled.

"I was just thinking how that old mule sure can eat collards," said the woman.

"Is it allowed to, I mean, eat someone's garden like that?" asked Alex.

"Ol' Belle? She can have all the collards she wants. She's earned it." The woman looked straight at Alex and said, "I let her loose, you see. And that's my garden. I thought I'd just sit in the shade and rest a bit before I shooed her out."

"But, ma'am, why do you let that mule eat your collard plants?"

"My name's Miz Pettway, son," she said. "What's yours?"

"I'm Alex," he answered.

"Well, Alex, there's enough greens in my garden for both of us. And Belle's a very special mule. She's a hero here in Gee's Bend. I like to show her some respect."

"What's so special about that old mule?" Alex asked as he stood up.

The woman took a deep breath. "Now, that's a long story. But if you have some time to sit . . ." She patted the bench.

Alex hesitated. He wondered if she was just a crazy old lady. But he was curious, and after all, there was nothing else to do.

"Gee's Bend has always been poor," she began. "There's not much here but farmland. We always needed mules to help us work the land. Not many of us could afford a car."

"How could you get anywhere?" Alex asked.

"Well, that's just it. Benders—that's what we call ourselves here—used mules to haul most everything. Belle's been with us for many years now. She was here the day Dr. Martin Luther King Jr. came to speak to us, way back in 1965."

"I know about Dr. Martin Luther King from school! Did you get to meet him?" Alex asked.

"Oh, yes, sir. I did! That night there was a terrible storm. Lots of people thought he wouldn't make it to see us poor folks. I waited not far from here with Belle. It was past midnight when Dr. King finally arrived. But he still spoke to us that night, and nearly took the roof off Pleasant Grove Baptist Church with his wonderful words!"

"What did he say?" Alex asked.

"Well, in those days, we had a ferry to cross the river into Camden, where there were jobs and stores. Dr. King told us to take the ferry to Camden and register to vote. 'Cross the river for freedom,' he sang out that night. Even though we were poor dirt farmers, descendants of slaves, with only mules to carry our loads, he said, 'I come over here to Gee's Bend to tell you — you are somebody!' He told us we had a right to vote.

"You understand, Alex, back then, no black person from Wilcox County had ever dared to vote."

"Were you scared?" Alex asked.

Miz Pettway sighed and thought for a moment. "I don't think we were scared—not after Dr. King spoke to us. We felt strong, like our mules. And we did just what he told us to do. So many went to register that we almost swamped that little ferry. Some Benders went on to march with Dr. King in Selma, in Montgomery, in Birmingham, and in the march on Washington. Benders are loyal, like mules, too," Miz Pettway added, chuckling.

"We read about all those marches in school!" Alex added.

"Mm-hm. But we must have scared the white folks in Camden, because the next thing we knew, they shut down the ferry. The white sheriff was a big bully who wanted to keep us in our place. He told reporters, 'We didn't close the ferry because they were black. We closed it because they *forgot* they were black.'

"So when it came time to vote, we had no way to cross the river. But we wouldn't be stopped. Benders are like ol' Belle here—not fancy, but strong and steady, and stubborn! We filled our few cars with as many people as could fit. And then our mules carried wagonloads of people 'round the river all day to vote. It took half a day to get there, but it was worth it. We sang and clapped all the way into town. Folks in Camden sure were surprised!"

"You showed them!" Alex laughed. "Is that why Belle's your hero?"

"There is more to it. A lot of people here lost their jobs in Camden because they voted. Things got bad. With no jobs, we had no money for food. So some of us joined the Freedom Quilting Bee in Alberta, and eventually we started our own. Called ourselves the Gee's Bend Quilters. You see, the women of Gee's Bend had always made quilts. Some of the most beautiful quilts in the world were made right here. Soon, they were being sold all over the United States. We became famous."

"That's why I'm here! My mother came here to shop for a quilt today," Alex explained. "That's a happy ending, isn't it?"

"But it's not the end of the story for Belle." Miz Pettway's voice turned softer. "Alex, do you remember learning in school what happened on the fourth of April in 1968?"

Alex looked into Miz Pettway's eyes and saw how sad they looked. "That's when Dr. King got shot, isn't it?" he asked, and for the first time he felt the sadness himself.

"Yes. Everyone in Gee's Bend was grieved." Miz Pettway took a deep breath and looked out at the trees. A slight breeze seemed to shuffle the leaves.

"We got a phone call, asking if our mules could pull Dr. King's coffin through the streets of Atlanta during the funeral parade. They wanted to use our mules, not fancy draft horses. Mules take their time, work hard, and they never back down. Mules aren't pretty, but they are somebody! It meant so much to us that Benders could honor the memory of Dr. King.

"Belle and another mule named Ada were loaded onto a truck to begin their journey to Atlanta. But as usual, it wasn't going to be easy. State policemen stopped the truck and asked the drivers to show them a permit for hauling livestock across state lines. They threatened to arrest the drivers when they didn't have the papers. Told them they'd have to turn back.

"We got the word to Dr. King's headquarters in Atlanta about what had happened, and they called the state police and the governors of Alabama and Georgia. They told them it would look shameful on TV and in the news all over the nation if they refused to let our mules pull the funeral train. After that, the troopers escorted our Belle and Ada right into Atlanta."

"Belle pulled Dr. Martin Luther King's coffin?" Alex asked.

"Yes, sir. Belle and Ada bravely pulled that wagon three and a half miles through streets that were full of grieving, weeping people. As they passed, people reached out and touched the mules and the casket. Imagine the thousands of arms and hands reaching out to them. But they kept moving, slow and steady. They didn't back down or get scared, just kept going.

"The funeral was televised around the world. Sixty thousand people gathered around the Ebenezer Baptist Church, and tens of thousands more lined the streets. We were very proud! And that's why we love our last mule here at Gee's Bend, and why I let Belle eat all the collard greens she wants."

Alex and Miz Pettway turned to look at old Belle, who stopped her munching and looked up at them. They both laughed.

"Yep, she's had her fill," Miz Pettway said, slowly rising off the bench. "Want to go meet her?"

"Yes, ma'am." Alex skipped down the steps and over to Belle, who let him scratch her fuzzy ears. Alex looked into the mule's eyes and thought about all the history she had seen. "Thank you for telling me about Belle," Alex said.

"Now you know what Dr. King meant when he told us that even though we led simple, hard lives, we were still somebody," she said.

"And even an old mule can be a hero," Alex added. Miz Pettway smiled and walked away, leading Belle behind her.

AUTHOR'S NOTE

I first heard the story of Belle from the Reverend James E. Orange, who had been working for Martin Luther King Jr. when the civil rights leader was assassinated on April 4, 1968. It had been Dr. King's wish that mules pull the farm wagon that would hold his burial casket. He had spent his life working to improve the lives of poor black people. The mules would be a powerful symbol.

Reverend Orange had the job of finding the mules. He remembered that King had spoken at Gee's Bend on several occasions and that members of the community had marched in protest with him elsewhere. He knew that Dr. King had long admired the "Benders," who lived simply and had faced hard times.

The people of Gee's Bend and their mules would play a big part in Martin Luther King Jr.'s history, just as he had in theirs. Indeed, one of the first African Americans to cast his vote after the passage of the National Voting Rights Act of 1965 was in Camden, Alabama. A few years later, Camden elected the first black sheriff of the twentieth century.

When news of King's assassination came, the Benders readily agreed to send two mules—Belle and Ada. The animals were loaded into a pickup and began the journey. The truck was stopped at the state border. When the driver could not produce a permit to ship livestock, he was refused permission to drive on to Atlanta.

Phone calls were made from King's staff to the governors of both Alabama and Georgia to ask for assistance. Knowing that this action threatened to delay the funeral and make national news, the two governors agreed that the Benders would be allowed to drive the mules on to Atlanta.

On April 9, 1968, Belle and Ada pulled the humble funeral wagon on a long, slow trek from Ebenezer Baptist Church to Morehouse College, where one of King's teachers, Reverend Benjamin Mays, delivered his eulogy. It is estimated that fifty thousand people marched in quiet procession behind the wagon. Belle and Ada had completed their part in the history of this great man.

—Calvin Alexander Ramsey

To the memory of Reverend James E. Orange, civil rights activist,
top aide to Martin Luther King Jr., and my friend, who empowered many
young African Americans and addressed everyone as "Leader."
C. A. R.

To all of my family and friends for your love and support.
Thank you for allowing me to live my passion.
J. H.

Text copyright © 2011 by Calvin Alexander Ramsey and Bettye Stroud
Illustrations copyright © 2011 by John Holyfield
Story developed by Pinafore Press

First paperback edition 2016

The Library of Congress has cataloged the hardcover edition as follows:

Ramsey, Calvin A.
Belle, the last mule at Gee's Bend / Calvin Alexander Ramsey and Bettye Stroud ; illustrated
by John Holyfield. — 1st ed.
p. cm.
Summary: In Gee's Bend, Alabama, Miz Pettway tells young Alex about the historic role her mule played
in the struggle for civil rights led by Dr. Martin Luther King, Jr. Includes factual information about the
community of Gee's Bend and Martin Luther King, Jr.
ISBN 978-0-7636-4058-3 (hardcover)
[1. Mules—Fiction. 2. Civil rights movements—Fiction. 3. King, Martin Luther, Jr., 1929–1968—Fiction.
4. African Americans—Fiction. 5. Alabama—History—1951—Fiction.] I. Stroud, Bettye, date,
II. Holyfield, John, ill. III. Title.
PZ7.R145Be 2011
[E]—dc22   2010048132

ISBN 978-0-7636-8769-4 (paperback)

19 20 21 APS 10 9 8 7 6 5

Printed in Humen, Dongguan, China

This book was typeset in Horley Old Style.
The illustrations were done in acrylics.

Candlewick Press
99 Dover Street
Somerville, Massachusetts 02144

visit us at www.candlewick.com